CHOPIN

14 OF HIS EASIEST PIANO SELECTIONS

A PRACTICAL PERFORMING EDITION

FREDERIC CHOPIN
A drawing from life by F. X. Winterhalter.

Contents

Selections are placed in approximate order of difficulty.

CANTABILE IN Bb MAJOR (Posthumous) 32

LARGO IN Eb MAJOR (Posthumous) 17

MAZURKA IN A MINOR, Op. 67, No. 4 (Posthumous) 10

MAZURKA IN Bb MAJOR, Op. 7, No. 1 28

MAZURKA IN C MAJOR, Op. 7, No. 5 16

MAZURKA IN C MAJOR, Op. 67, No. 3 (Posthumous) 8

MAZURKA IN F MAJOR, Op. 68, No. 3 (Posthumous) 13

MAZURKA IN G MINOR, Op. 67, No. 2 (Posthumous) 26

PRELUDE IN A MAJOR, Op. 28, No. 7 22

PRELUDE IN B MINOR, Op. 28, No. 6 20

PRELUDE IN E MINOR, Op. 28, No. 4 18

WALTZ IN A MINOR (Posthumous) 3

WALTZ IN B MINOR, Op. 69, No. 2 (Posthumous) 23

WALTZ IN Eb MAJOR (Posthumous) 6

Copyright © MCMXCV by Alfred Publishing Co., Inc.
All rights reserved. Printed in USA.

Book Alone
ISBN-10: 0-7390-2228-8
ISBN-13: 978-0-7390-2228-3

Book & CD
ISBN-10: 0-7390-4753-1
ISBN-13: 978-0-7390-4753-8

Cover art: A detail from Place de la Concord, *ca. 1837*
by William Wyld (English, 1806–1889)
Courtesy of Art Resource, New York

Portrait by Eugene Delacroix

FREDERIC CHOPIN

In a little village near Warsaw on February 22, 1810, a child was born whose natural musical gifts rivaled those of Mozart. He was, like Mozart, destined for a short life. He was also destined to revolutionize the art of composing for the piano. His name was Frederic Francois Chopin.

The young Chopin heard music from the day of his birth, played by his mother and by his sister, Louise, on a real grand piano. The effects of this music on the child were overwhelming. He was irresistably drawn to the keyboard. By the time he was six, he was amazing all who heard him with his improvisations. His parents placed him with an excellent teacher, Wojciech Zywny, who introduced him to the music of J. S. Bach, Mozart, Haydn, Beethoven, and other masters. When he was only seven, his first published composition, a *Polonaise in G minor,* was billed as a work of true genius.

Chopin entered the Conservatory in Warsaw at the age of 12 and, under the guidance of Josef Elsner, he developed as a composer, graduating at the age of 19. By the time he was 20 years old, he had written nearly fifty compositions for piano as well as many songs and works for other instruments.

While he was yet only 19 years old, Chopin made his debut in Vienna, causing great commotion among the musical elite of that great center of the arts. Schumann hailed him as a genius, Mendelssohn praised his playing, but he considered his compositions rather strange for his own conservative tastes. Although his concert debut in 1829 was a great success, Chopin did not appear in public frequently during his lifetime. When he did, he preferred to play at musicales for small audiences. He lacked the dazzling showmanship that the European public had learned to enjoy and expect, and he rebelled against that type of performance. He made his living through the success of his compositions, which were played by all the great concert artists of his day, and which were eagerly awaited by the publishers. Often his pieces were printed simultaneously by publishers in England, France, and Germany, and scholars have a difficult time determining which of these printings represent a "first edition."

Chopin composed over 200 piano compositions in large and small forms, most of which are still part of the active repertoire of concert artists the world over. Although he did not, during his lifetime, enjoy fame equal to that of Mendelssohn, Liszt, or even Kalkbrenner and Hummel, today his piano works are performed more frequently than those of any of his contemporaries. He was the greatest of the romanticists (though he detested the word) and the first modernist. His innovations in pedaling and fingering, along with his introduction of new elements of style in playing, were to raise the art of the piano to a new pinnacle.

All of Chopin's great works were completed in a lifespan of only 39 years. He died October 17, 1849.

Fortunately, not all of Chopin's works, even in their original versions, are difficult. Chopin was in the habit of writing down short pieces for his friends. Many of these have been discovered only recently, and although they are quite simple, they are still Chopin and they bear the stamp of his genius for composing beautiful, expressive melodies. The pieces selected for this book are the very easiest of all of Chopin's compositions, and they are presented here in their original form, without simplification. They should provide many hours of enjoyment and at the same time an opportunity for many pianists to become acquainted with the works of this brilliant master composer.

During his lifetime, Chopin was probably best known for his waltzes. It is said that no musicale was considered complete without the performance of one or more of the brilliant *grand valses*. This short waltz, discovered only recently, is probably the simplest of Chopin's compositions in this form. It nevertheless bears the unmistakable stamp of Chopin's great genius for composing elegant, expressive melodies.

WALTZ IN A MINOR

Posthumous

The original manuscript of this work, the shortest of all of Chopin's waltzes, was discovered only in 1941 by Dr. Jacques Chailley, of the Paris Conservatoire. Originally the piece bore no title except for the dedication to his friend and pupil, Emile Gaillard.

WALTZ IN E♭ MAJOR

to Emile Gaillard

Posthumous

The *mazurka* is one of the traditional national dances of Poland. It always has three beats in a measure, and there is a certain accentuation of the second beat that is characteristic of its correct performance. This mazurka is an excellent representation of the mazurka as a piece for dancing. Chopin wrote over fifty mazurkas for the piano, bringing many refinements to the form and style.

MAZURKA IN C MAJOR

pour M-e. Hoffman

Op. 67, No. 3
Posthumous

D. S. 𝄋 al Fine

MAZURKA IN A MINOR

Op. 67, No. 4
Posthumous

* Small hands may omit small notes.

Fine

D. S. 𝄋 al Fine

MAZURKA IN F MAJOR

Op. 68, No. 3
Posthumous

Fine

Poco piu vivo

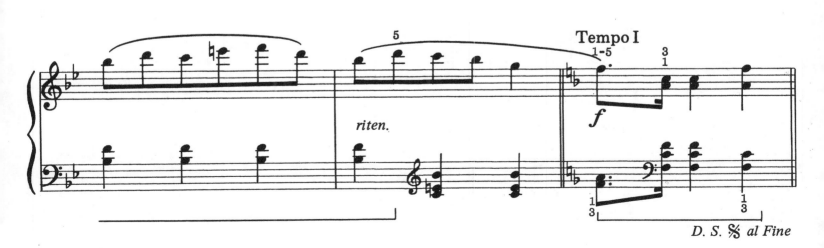

D. S. 𝄋 al Fine

This is the shortest of all of Chopin's mazurkas . . . or perhaps the longest. The performer is free to repeat it as many times as desired. The instructions at the end, *Dal Segno 𝄋 Senza Fine,* mean "repeat from the sign 𝄋 without ending."

MAZURKA IN C MAJOR

à Monsieur Johns de la Nouvelle Orléans

Op. 7, No. 5

D. S. 𝄋 Senza Fine

The original manuscript of this beautiful piece was discovered only a few years ago. It is in the library of the Paris Conservatoire. Play it legato throughout, very slowly and with much expression.

LARGO IN E♭ MAJOR

Posthumous

The *Twenty-Four Preludes, Opus 28,* were completed in the halls and rooms of an old monastery in Majorca in 1839. They have been praised as the very finest of Chopin's compositions by no less a critic than Robert Schumann. Of this, the fourth prelude, the great musical educator Friedrich Niecks wrote, "This is an exquisite little poem, the languid pensiveness of which defies description. It seems to shut out the wide, noisy world, for a time."

PRELUDE IN E MINOR

Op. 28, No. 4

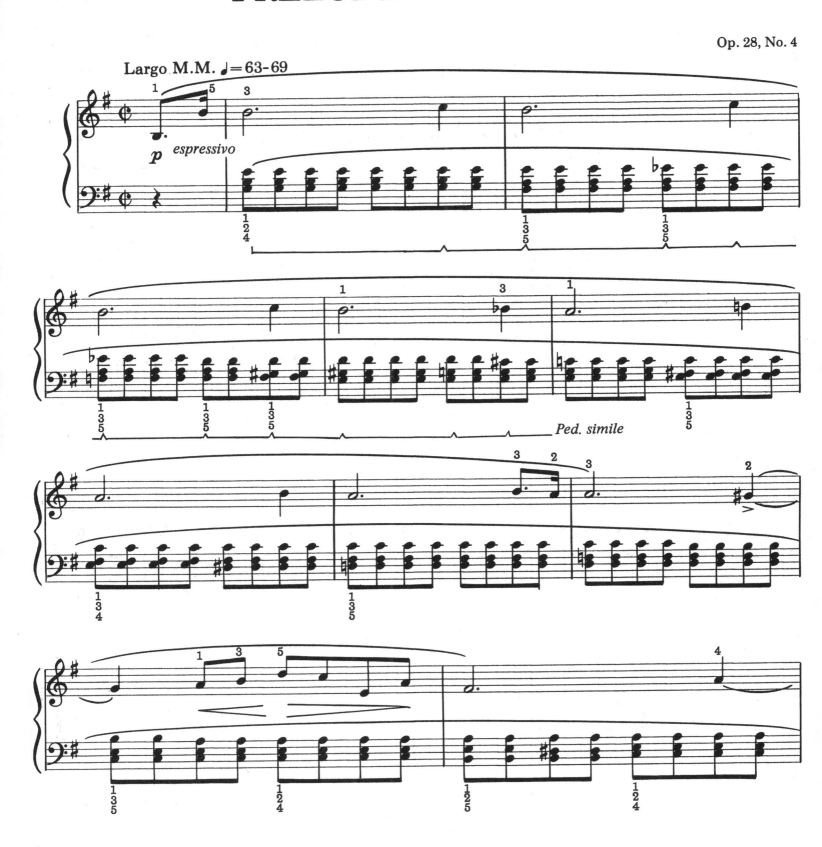

A wonderful melodic study for the left hand, this prelude is artfully constructed, along classical lines. The echo effect on page 21 is skillfully managed. It should be played very expressively, with a very slow tempo, and without a trace of monotony.

PRELUDE IN B MINOR

à son ami J. C. Kessler

Op. 28, No. 6

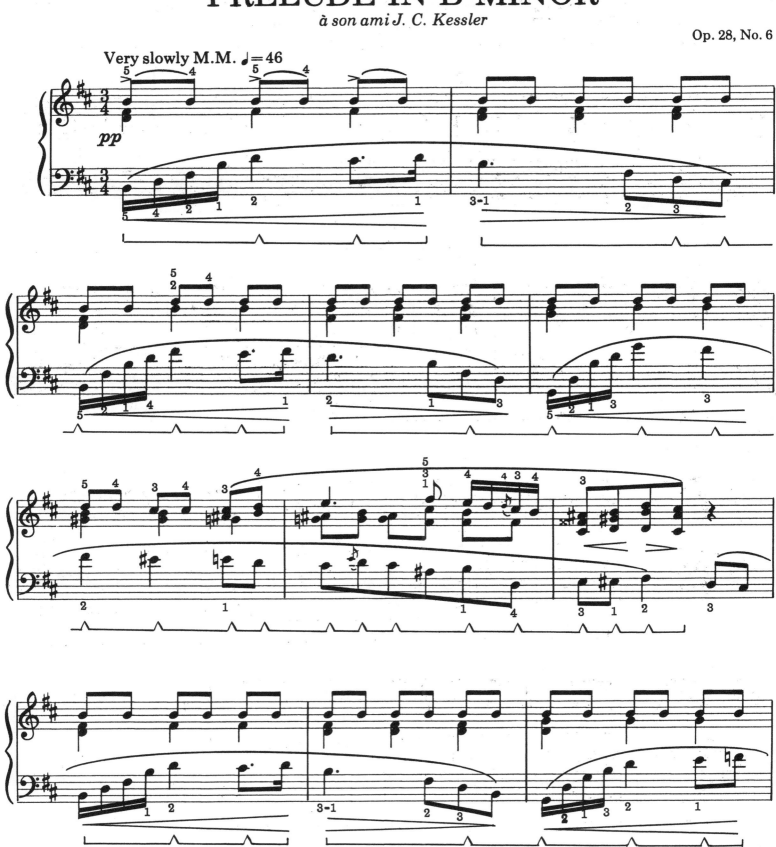

PRELUDE IN A MAJOR

à son ami J. C. Kessler

Op. 28, No. 7

* Students with small hands may wish to use one of the following simplifications:

This is the easiest of two versions of this famous waltz. The original includes a more difficult trio, in F sharp major. This version is taken from an original manuscript, written in Chopin's own hand.

WALTZ IN B MINOR

Op. 69, No. 2
Posthumous

Although this is another of Chopin's short mazurkas, it is among the most beautiful. According to Chopin's close friend, Jules Fontana, who published this work shortly after Chopin's death, it was written in 1849, the last year of Chopin's life.

MAZURKA IN G MINOR

Op. 67, No. 2
Posthumous

D. S. 𝄋 al Fine

This is the most popular of all mazurkas. Of this work Chopin's biographer, James Huneker, wrote, "It has an air of elegance that is alluring. It is a jolly, reckless composition that makes one happy to be alive and dancing."

MAZURKA IN B♭ MAJOR

a Monsieur Johns de la Nouvelle Orléans

Op. 7, No. 1

This short piece is similar in effect to a miniature nocturne, and is excellent preparation for learning the larger works in that form. It should be played very freely and with much expression.

CANTABILE IN B♭ MAJOR

Posthumous